Marge
in
Charge

Isla Fisher has worked in TV and film for 25 years. She has played many fun and different characters, but her favourite role is being a mummy to her three children. Isla has been making up bedtime stories for them every night since they were born, which is how *Marge in Charge* began.

Eglantine Ceulemans spent her childhood reading Belgian comics. She loves combining humour and sensitivity, and using different media and techniques. Eglantine currently resides in Lyon.

Marge
in
Charge

ISLA FISHER
Illustrated by Eglantine Ceulemans

Piccadilly
PRESS

First published in Great Britain in 2016 by
PICCADILLY PRESS
80–81 Wimpole St, London W1G 9RE
www.piccadillypress.co.uk

Text copyright © Isla Fisher, 2016
Illustrations copyright © Eglantine Ceulemans, 2016

A CIP catalogue record for this book is available from the British Library.

ISBN: 978-1-84812-533-9
also available as an ebook

10

Printed and bound by Clays Ltd, Elcograf S.p.A.

Piccadilly Press is an imprint of Bonnier Publishing Fiction,
a Bonnier Publishing company
www.bonnierpublishingfiction.co.uk
www.bonnierpublishing.co.uk

For Olive, Elula and Monty.
My favourite small people on the planet
and the best editors a writer could wish for.

the Button Family

Mum

Dad

Jake

Me
(Jemima)

Marge
Babysits

My name is Jemima Button. I am seven years old and I'm the tallest girl in my class. My little brother is Jakeypants, though grown-ups call him Jake, and he is four years old. He loves wrestling, dinosaurs and ice cream.

We live with our mummy and daddy in an ordinary house, on an ordinary street. We used to be an ordinary family until the day our babysitter came.

It was five o'clock on Thursday, and our family was sitting around the table. Our parents were dressed up in their smart clothes.

'Why do we need a babysitter?' asks Jake.

'Because we are going out for dinner,' explains Daddy, patting Jakeypants on the head.

Mummy smiles and says, 'We need someone here to look after you.'

I can see that my baby brother is not happy. He begins to cry – well, fake cry. He wails and flails his arms around like a baby penguin on slippery ice.

'Do you want to read a story?' asks Daddy, handing Jake his favourite book.

'Stupid book!' says Jake and throws it on the ground.

Oh no. I bite my lip. When Jakeypants starts throwing things it means he is headed for a tantrum. What will our new babysitter think? The last time we had a babysitter Jake spent the whole time hiding in his room building a Lego weapon so that he could 'destroy' her! He was cross at her because she scolded him for covering Daddy's desk with stickers. And then I had to peel them all off!

I hope Jakey behaves himself tonight. He can be very stubborn and naughty when he wants to be.

'There's your favourite for dinner: macaroni cheese,' says Mummy, as she puts it into the fridge. Jake's face lights up, but not for long.

'. . . and broccoli,' he adds, scowling. 'I don't want broccoli and I definitely do NOT want a babysitter,' Jake shouts.

'Even if the broccoli is on your blue T. rex plate?' Mummy pleads.

'Especially then!' Jakey retorts.

Mummy gives Daddy a panicked look.

Everyone knows that my little brother has two rules:

1. He won't wash his hair — he says it's 'boring'

2. He won't eat broccoli. Ever

6

But then we meet someone extraordinary: our new babysitter.

DING DONG, that's the doorbell.

Straight away Jakey stops crying and races to the door. He peeks through the window then takes off his shorts and pulls them over his head. Jake always does this when he wants to wrestle or stop someone from coming in the house, like Uncle Desmond.

'Put your shorts back on,' Mummy says sternly. Daddy is opening the door.

'Meet Marge!' Daddy says in the voice he saves for his boss at work.

I peep from behind Daddy as I always feel shy around new grown-ups.

There she is – Marge, the babysitter!

Standing in our hallway is a person so small that she only comes up to Daddy's armpit! She is wearing a little yellow woolly hat and reading glasses.

Her face looks serious too and I worry that she will be strict, like my nursery teacher Mrs Ratley, who made us eat all our packed lunch even when the sandwiches were soggy.

She has a big round belly and skinny legs with knees as knobbly as twigs.

'Hi, Marge,' I say and give her my bravest smile.

But Jake has only noticed how small Marge is. She is definitely NOT tall enough to ride a rollercoaster. She could even fit in Jake's cardboard box that he uses as his superhero hideout.

'Are you a kid or a grown-up?' he asks, peering closely at her.

'Definitely a grown-up,' answers Marge gleefully.

'Then why are you so small?' demands Jake.

'Well, why are YOU so small?' asks Marge right back.

'Because I'm only four years old!' Jake rolls his eyes. He is brilliant at eye rolling even though Mummy told him that it's rude to do it to grown-ups. 'You look one hundred years old,' he snorts.

Mummy and Daddy look worried that Marge will be offended but instead she throws her head back and laughs. This makes me feel a little bit less nervous, so I say, 'I'm Jemima.'

'Nice to meet you,' Marge says solemnly, shaking my hand like adults do. It makes me giggle.

'Are you a Christmas elf?' asks Jake. 'Let me see if your ears are pointy.' Jake is now peering at the sides of Marge's head. Daddy coughs nervously and steers Jake away from Marge.

'The rules are on the fridge,' Mummy tells Marge. 'If you have any questions ask Jemima, she's my big girl. We will be back by eight o'clock.' Then she turns to us. 'Remember to be polite and say "please" and "thank you" when Marge takes care of you.'

'We will,' I promise.

I hear Mummy telling Marge that it's very important for Jake to eat all his dinner, especially the broccoli, and wondering if she could possibly try washing his hair? Then she gives Marge the number of her mobile phone for emergencies.

Mummy and Daddy both give me a big hug. The butterflies in my belly aren't so fluttery now that we've met Marge. I am very curious about her, but still nervous that my little brother might misbehave.

To my surprise, though, he lets Mummy hug him goodbye, which he never normally does.

We stand on the doorstep either side of Marge and wave as my parents leave. The minute the car has gone, we head inside.

'Are you a dwarf? From *Snow White*?' Jakey asks.

'No, and I'm not an Oompa-Loompa either,' laughs Marge.

'Oompa-Loompas only exist in *Charlie and the Chocolate Factory*,' I say.

'Are you a jockey? Do you gallop horses in a race?' Jake asks.

Marge shakes her head.

'Did you drive here? How did your little feet reach the pedals?' asks Jake.

'I am sure you can lower the steering wheel!' I offer helpfully.

'I actually use a booster chair,' Marge says.

Then she leans in secretively.

'Being small means I can visit the museum half price!' she brags as she takes off her glasses and pea-green coat. Then Marge pulls off her hat. Guess what's underneath? Long colourful hair that falls halfway down her back! Green, blue, orange, red and yellow hair like a waterfall of colour.

I wonder if Mummy would let Marge look after us if she saw her crazy hair!

'Wow!' I say. Marge crosses her feet underneath her and exhales.

'I was born Margery Beauregard Victoria Ponterfois, and I am a duchess.'

'A duchess?' I ask, blinking. 'Are you Dutch?'

Marge laughs, and little creases form beside her blue eyes.

'No. The King of England's fourth son is my uncle Leonard.'

'Do you have any children?' I ask.

Marge shakes her head.

'But I have ten pets: three white miniature ponies, three swans, two polka-dot Pomeranian puppies, a cheeky long-tooth ferret and an albino water buffalo.'

I can barely breathe with excitement.

'I used to live at the palace but the royal guards wouldn't allow my pets to sleep in my bed. Did you know that there are 779 rooms at the royal palace? I was always getting lost. Sometimes I would fall asleep looking for my bedroom! So my pet friends and I set out on an adventure to find a new home.'

NORTH POLE: Alfie, Alvin & Arnoldo the swans are not happy with new home: too cold.

Jakey is behaving really well and I can tell that he's enjoying Marge's story.

'Have you ever been on a bus?' Jakey asks. He is obsessed with buses.

'Of course,' sniffs Marge. 'I have ridden a red double decker bus, an airport bus and a minibus . . .'

WOW! Jakey is really impressed with Marge now.

' . . . but my favourite mode of transport is the royal coach pulled by eight palomino donkeys.'

I want to ask Marge all sorts of questions about her animal friends and her life, but suddenly she jumps up and says: 'Now, your mummy wants me to read the rules on the fridge. Hop to it!'

We follow her to the kitchen, and Marge reads the list aloud:

1. Dinner is at 5.30. There's macaroni cheese and broccoli in the fridge

2. Playtime next but all toys must be put away afterwards

3. Bath time is at 6.30 and please try to wash Jake's hair

4. Bed by 7.30

I would much rather listen to more of Marge's story, but Marge is looking very serious now that she has read Mummy's list. 'I think we might need to add a few new dinner rules,' she says.

Jake groans, and my stomach sinks.

'I won't eat broccoli. Not now, not ever,' says my brother haughtily.

Marge just raises one eyebrow and she grabs a napkin and folds it as she says, 'I have been to many exotic dinners all around the world. I have dined with princesses, knights, lords and ladies and I have my own royal dinner-making rules,' says Marge as she finishes crafting the napkin into a splendid chef's hat and pops it onto her own head.

Jake and I exchange an excited look. Cooking? Our new babysitter is going to let us cook! I race to the bottom drawer and find our aprons. We quickly put them on and tie the bows.

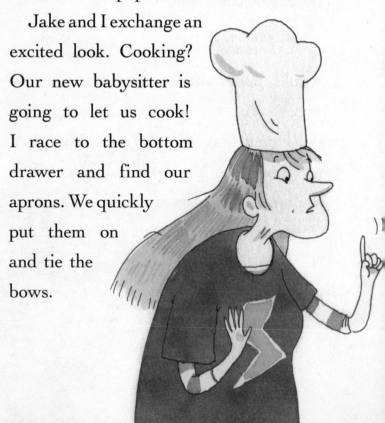

'Right, let's see . . .' says Chef Marge. '. . . *Rule One: prepare the food.* Jemima, you will be the chef's helper.' I have no idea what that is but I begin gathering all the ingredients that Marge tells me to and Marge informs Jakey that he will be the waiter.

'Do waiters get to wrestle?' Jake karate kicks the air.

'Yes. But first they have to ask the dinner party guests what they want for dinner and write it down in this little pad.' She hands a notebook and a silver pen to Jake.

'But I can't write any words yet – except for my name,' Jake sighs.

'Don't worry,' says Marge, 'I read squiggles! I can even read the handwriting of all my pets – how else do you think we communicate?'

WOW! I have always wondered whether chickens could handwrite, or rather claw-write.

'It all started when my camel asked me to translate a love letter she had received from a dairy cow. Now that was tough, because cows don't use their hooves for writing . . .'

'What do they use then?' asks Jake curiously.

'Their tails, of course!' cries Marge. Then she gives Jakey and me a bowl. 'You know, Prince Leonard won the heart of my aunt with a red velvet birthday cake. Baron Dinklestitch wasn't pleased, mind you . . .'

Jake and I crack eight eggs into a bowl. Jakey accidentally drops in half of the shell but we just cover it in a pile of flour. Then we add a mountain of cereal and a teabag for good measure. Marge tells us she thinks that we are very creative chefs but I am not sure that Mummy would agree with that.

Once everything is cooking nicely Marge gets the list out again and adds another new rule.

Rule Two: lay the table.

Jake groans. But Marge tells us it's the only way to decide on our guest list for the dinner party.

21

'You mean we're inviting guests to eat with us?' I ask.

'Of course!' she replies. 'Dinner should always be a dinner party, and the perfect number for a dinner party is six.'

So we decide to include Archie, our pug-nosed puppy dog, but we still only have four!

'We will lay the table for six anyway and maybe some special guests will surprise us,' Marge says.

We place three plates and three forks and knives for every guest but because Archie can't use cutlery I give him a pair of chopsticks.

'What's next on Mummy's list?' I ask Marge, hoping she'll have some more extra rules.

Marge toots a pretend trumpet.

... Rule Three: decorate the dining room!

Soon we are cutting out cardboard stars and making streamers and Jake staples the stars onto the tablecloth. Then he gets carried away and staples his T-shirt to his shorts and staples one of his socks to a tea towel, and he is about to actually staple Archie's tail to his leg when Marge swoops in.

'Can I borrow the stapler?' Marge asks quickly and then hides it instantly.

Jake sticky tapes Pete, his toy stegosaurus, to the centre of the table as a decoration and we tie a ribbon on the back of everyone's chair. I only just learned how to tie a bow and I can do it quite quickly now.

'A room fit for kings and queens!' Marge says and high fives us both. 'And perfect for a duchess. It's all ready for dinner now.'

PHEW! My tummy is making funny grumbly sounds and I can smell our cake baking in the kitchen but then Marge checks the list again.

'It's time to get cleaned up so we can look fabulous for our dinner party,' Marge says, blowing the whistle hard. 'Bathtime!'

Bathtime before supper? This is very unusual but Marge is in charge, so we follow her upstairs.

In the bathroom Jake refuses to run the bath or fetch his towel. I am worried because I know how stubborn my little brother can be, but Marge has a fun idea. She fills the sink with water all the way to the top, and empties in a *whole* bottle of lavender bubble bath. It's incredible – bubbles are floating serenely onto the floor and covering our toes.

Then she tips in a bottle of apple shampoo,

Daddy's aftershave, Mummy's face cream and she even sprays in some fancy perfume.

Jakey holds his nose 'Phew-eee,' he says, giggling.

Then she somehow finds our swimming goggles, which have been lost for ages, and we put them on. Marge has a whistle. 'It's time to dunk!' she cries, blowing the whistle hard. 'One, two, three –

DUNK!'

Jakey and I plunge our heads in the sink and under the taps, then up again. Soon we are surrounded by bubbles floating under our chins and around our ears! Jakey makes a white Santa beard and I make a white wig of foamy bubbles.

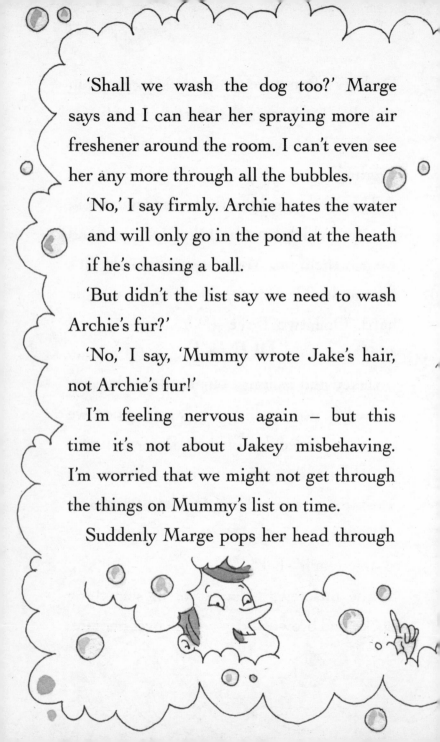

'Shall we wash the dog too?' Marge says and I can hear her spraying more air freshener around the room. I can't even see her any more through all the bubbles.

'No,' I say firmly. Archie hates the water and will only go in the pond at the heath if he's chasing a ball.

'But didn't the list say we need to wash Archie's fur?'

'No,' I say, 'Mummy wrote Jake's hair, not Archie's fur!'

I'm feeling nervous again – but this time it's not about Jakey misbehaving. I'm worried that we might not get through the things on Mummy's list on time.

Suddenly Marge pops her head through

the bubbles and grins at us before turning to Jake. 'Do you want a shampoo mohican?'

Jake nods, although neither of us even know what a mohican is! Marge lathers up Jake's hair with shampoo until it stands in one point on top of his head. He looks hilarious, like a white rooster. Then she lathers up mine like an ice cream.

The bathroom is a bit of a mess, but Jake has clean hair and is happy and Mummy will be so happy too! I'm a bit worried, though – we've still got lots to do, and we haven't been following the list in order!

'What's this shelf?' Marge asks. I can vaguely see through the white fluffy clouds of foam that she has found Mummy's 'out-of-our-reach' shelf.

She unscrews a large pot of something sticky and brown and rubs it all over her face.

'This must be a mud mask, to tighten the pores of the skin,' Marge assumes. But I can read the label and it clearly says BROWN HAIR DYE.

Oh no! Marge has put hair dye all over her face. It's turning orange . . . She really does look like an Oompa-Loompa now!

'Quick, Marge, wipe it off!' I shout. 'That is not a face mask!'

I don't want Marge's face to be the same colour as Mummy's hair!

WHOOPEE! Marge plunges her face into the water in the sink and is scrubbing her cheeks! Now bubbles and water are all over the floor.

Archie trots into the bathroom and starts barking at Marge.

'I am Marge the Mermaid!' gurgles Marge as she pops back up.

'I told you she wasn't a real grown-up,' Jake whispers to me, looking around at the messy bathroom.

'Come on, Marge,' I say. 'It's time to get back to our list.'

I have to say it isn't easy finding Marge in those bubbles. They're everywhere, rising all the way up to the ceiling.

'Gotcha!' I say, grabbing her foot, but

31

then I lift it up and it's a bottle of shampoo!

'I have her elbow!' Jakey shouts and then holds up a bag of bath salts.

We both crack up laughing!

'Marge, is that you?' I say, pulling out a tub of body gel.

Finally I feel something moving and grab at her. She feels very hairy and furry and as I pull her out I realise I have Archie in my arms! How did Archie get into the sink?

'Boo!' shouts Marge through a curtain of foam, grinning from ear to ear.

Once we are dry, Marge has a new idea. 'What shall we wear to dinner?' she asks us, as if we are in charge, not her.

'Anything but shorts!' shouts Jake, his hair now clean and dry. Jakey HATES shorts. Even in summer.

'We can't wear ordinary clothes,' says our babysitter. 'Going to a dinner party is a regal affair and we have to look our best.'

I have an idea. 'I'll be right back!' I say and I run off to find our dressing-up box. When I get back I find Marge and Jakey in Mummy and Daddy's room.

They are standing right inside Mummy's closet, pulling out all her special evening gowns. Oh no! Mummy will not be happy if we make a mess and I don't want to get in trouble. But it does look like fun . . .

'You can borrow my fairy wings,' I offer Marge. 'And my ladybird Halloween costume will fit Jakey.'

Marge shakes her head and instead she puts on a pirate patch and gladiator sword.

'At a dinner party it's important that you stand out,' says Marge, buttoning Jake into a yellow sequinned jacket. 'I was at a dinner party in Paris when I caught the eye of the Earl of Toulouse and he taught me to tango.'

'What's tango?' Jake is squinting at Marge.

'I'll show you,' says Marge and she picks

my little brother up into a hug and dances him around the room, singing loudly.

'The Earl Of Toulouse taught me to dance like this but he had a rose between his teeth and a red monkey jacket on.' Marge looks giddy with the memory.

Jake and I catch each other's eyes as Marge warbles on and start laughing so much my chest hurts. Then I remember Mummy has a pink feather boa. It's really soft and silky and she lets me wear it if I am very careful.

It would look perfect with Marge's hair so I find the box and offer it to her.

'You should wear it,' says Marge kindly.

I finally choose a sparkly evening gown and tall heels to go with the feather boa. I also wear Mummy's gold bracelets looped over my ears – Marge says I look like a baroness. Jake matches Daddy's wellington boots with his sequinned jacket and a French beret.

Marge grabs Daddy's black dinner jacket and folds up the sleeves to fit her short arms. And she adds the suit trousers which are so long they drag along the ground. She even finds his black bow tie and a top hat. Then she grabs a black magic marker from her handbag and draws a twirly-whirly moustache on her face. Marge looks like a boy!

'Moustaches make gentlemen look mysterious!' she says, bowing and talking in a deep voice.

Marge and I admire ourselves in Mummy's large mirror and pretend we are on our way to a swish restaurant, until we are distracted by the noise of Jakey jumping dangerously fast off Mummy's bed.

'That looks fun!' says Marge, and she joins in.

Soon we are all jumping off the bed and I finally understand why Jakey does it all the time.

My legs are so tired they are wobbly and my tummy is really rumbling when Marge holds out the list and sings, 'It's time for the dinner party to commence!'

'Who are the special guests?' Jakey wants to know.

As we walk downstairs, I am struck by an utterly brilliant idea. I sneak back to my bedroom and return with a shoebox that has holes poked in the top.

'Ta-da!' I cry.
I lift the lid.

'Marge, meet Bill and Bob: our pet snails. They can be our special dinner guests!'

Marge looks very pleased and Jake is jumping up and down with excitement.

'Mummy says they have to stay in the box, but this is a special occasion and we need six guests,' I reason, lifting them out gently.

'They leave a shimmery trail behind them like gooey fairy dust!' Jakey marvels.

'Now we have our guests, we can start!' Marge says with a cheer.

Marge carries Archie to Jakey's old highchair and he sits there looking quite confused.

He is not normally even allowed to be in the dining room and now he is sitting at the table with two chopsticks in front of him!

Jake takes everyone's orders very politely, gives his notepad to Marge, then sits quietly in his chair. I have never seen him so well behaved or with such clean hair. If only Mummy could see him now!

There are a lot of banging and crashing sounds in the kitchen before Marge brings out one large bowl covered by a silver lid.

I'm really hungry now so I'm quite excited.

Marge lifts the lid dramatically and underneath there is a big bowl of brown goo and six spoons.

'Chef Marge has your starter!'

'I am *not* eating *that*!' Jakey says. He's looking a little bit grumpy – I think he might be hungry too.

'It's *Soup a la Chocolatay*,' Marge announces in a perfect French accent.

'It's not the hair dye again, is it?' I ask.

Our babysitter digs her spoon daintily into the 'soup' before taking a big **SLURRRP** from her bowl.

'It's chocolate soup,' she says proudly. 'I melted three whole bars, and five mini ones that I found in my handbag.'

Chocolate soup?

'Mummy never lets us eat chocolate unless it's a special treat,' I explain. Jake and I exchange a grin.

'Marge is in charge,' says Jake cheerfully as he spoons some chocolate soup into his mouth. I have never seen Jake eat anything with a spoon before – he normally uses his fingers.

My tummy is rumbling and the melted

chocolate smells delicious so I pick up a spoon and have a taste.

'Scrummy yummy in my tummy!' I say. That's what Grandpa Bert always says when he tastes anything delicious.

It's so tasty that before we know it Marge, Jakey and I are hugging the bowl between us and licking the inside and our fingers, and chocolate is everywhere and Marge tells us that unfortunately there isn't enough left for the other guests at the dinner party.

Oops! I forgot about our dinner guests. Bill and Bob have sloped away but Archie looks disappointed.

Marge goes back to the kitchen to get the next bit of the meal.

It feels like she is gone for a really long time and we are really hungry now.

Finally Marge returns with pasta. 'And

now for our main course!' she announces. It's dripping with the white cheese sauce which we both love.

Marge shows Jake and I which fork to use and how to look elegant while eating pasta. We twizzle and whirl our forks and listen to Marge. She tells us a story about when she was young and the Queen of England taught her to use cutlery for the first time.

Archie does not look elegant as he wolfs down his portion of pasta – there is cheese sauce all over his face. He licks it off.

SLURP! SLURP!

'And now for dessert,' says Marge after we have finished. She disappears into the kitchen and although I'm quite full now I can't wait to eat more delicious food.

But Marge has a surprise in store – she returns with two small bowls of broccoli.

Jake shakes his head suspiciously. 'That is NOT dessert. That is broccoli and I refuse to eat it!'

'You are right, it is broccoli,' says Marge, smiling. 'And we can't eat broccoli at the dinner table,' she adds.

What is she thinking? Eating our dinner was the first rule on Mummy's list.

'We can't eat broccoli ANYWHERE,' says Jake crossly.

'What about on a bus?' Marge asks innocently. 'Would you eat broccoli on a bus?' Jakey's eyes widen as Marge drags over the cardboard box that he uses as his superhero hideout. She pulls four tiny chairs out from the playroom and puts them in two rows in the box, just like the inside of a bus!

Then she crawls inside the box and squeezes into the driver's seat!

'All aboard the bus, please,' she calls.

Jakey mimes giving Marge his ticket, then races inside the box and takes a seat happily. I bring over our bowls and sit down next to my brother. I nibble on my broccoli and pretend to wave out of the bus window.

Would you believe it, Jakey eats all his broccoli! Mummy will be thrilled.

Not only has Jake eaten his broccoli but he's used a fork and a spoon and his hair is clean.

Marge looks happy too as she checks everything off the list and sighs.

'After a royal banquet or dinner party, the guests retire into the living room to chat,' Marge explains. She curls up in Daddy's armchair.

Jakey and I snuggle up on the sofa. I don't even mind when Jakey leans his head on me.

'Don't you miss the palace?' I ask. I saw the changing of the guards at Buckingham Palace once, and I would love to go inside.

'Never!' retorts Marge. 'I left to travel the world seeking wild adventures in faraway lands!'

'Have you ever babysat before?' I ask.

'No. I am usually very, incredibly, always, typically . . . busy,' Marge replies with a yawn.

'What do you do for a job?' Jakey asks.

'Well, I try to take my puppies roller-skating every day, my ferret has an enormous hat collection and insists on trying them all on each morning and my ponies like me to tell them stories while braiding their tails – and those are only half of my jobs,' says Marge sleepily.

It's getting dark outside and I realise that it's probably past our bedtime, and Mummy and Daddy will soon be home. I think about the messy kitchen, Mummy's closet and the bathroom full of bubbles. Marge notices my expression. She looks tired.

'The cleaner will be here shortly, I'm sure.'

'Er, Marge . . .' I don't know how to break it to her. 'Marge – we don't have a cleaner!'

'What about a maid?' Marge asks, yawning.

I shake my head, no.

'A butler?' Marge's eyelids are drooping.

Again, I shake my head.

'Not even a chambermaid?' she mumbles sleepily.

'No,' I say. I don't even know what a chambermaid is!

But Marge has fallen asleep. Her skinny legs are poking out from underneath her belly as it rises and falls with each snore.

I check the clock and it's five to eight. Uh-oh. We are going to be in *big* trouble. My stomach feels quivery.

'Jake, we only have five minutes till Mummy and Daddy come back!' I whisper, so as not to wake our babysitter.

Jake jumps up in shock.

'We have to clean everything up or Mummy and Daddy won't let Marge come and look after us again!'

My little brother is looking at me with big worried eyes. 'Let's tidy, NOW!' he whispers back urgently.

I can't believe it because Jakey HATES tidying up! He must really like our new babysitter.

We rush from room to room like little whirlwinds. The whole house is a disaster zone. There are towels and bubbles on the bathroom floor, Mummy's clothes are thrown around the living room and the kitchen sink is piled up with chocolatey bowls. Marge is still fast asleep in Daddy's armchair. Her messy rainbow hair is spread out and she still has a black marker moustache and chocolate around her mouth.

Gently I wake her up. 'Marge, it's time to clean your face and brush your hair before Mummy and Daddy get back. We'll tidy the house.' She smiles sleepily at me and shuffles off towards the downstairs toilet.

Then I run around picking up Mummy's clothes while Jake grabs the mop and starts on the bathroom floor. I rinse the dishes and leave them in a sink full of hot, bubbly water. Jake puts Mummy's make-up away and I

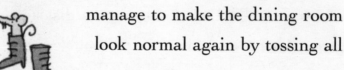

manage to make the dining room look normal again by tossing all our decorations into the laundry basket.

'Marge?' I call, wondering if she's finished getting ready. But she doesn't reply and I can't see her anywhere downstairs – our babysitter has disappeared!

There's no time to find her – I can hear Mummy and Daddy at the front door.

Quickly, we bolt upstairs to our bedroom. Archie is curled up sleeping on the rug in our room. Whyever is he not sleeping in his own doggy bed? I scramble onto my top bunk and Jakey flings himself onto the bottom bunk just as Mummy creaks opens our bedroom door.

I give a snorting sound which I hope Mummy will think is a snore.

Mummy and Daddy kiss our faces softly as we pretend to be sleeping.

'They're fast asleep,' she whispers to Daddy.

I hear them move towards the door.

'Is that Bob on the table?' she asks.

I open an eye. Oh no!

'Oh, and there's Bill,'

says Dad. 'They must have

got loose, but how did they get upstairs?'

Mum picks up Bob and Bill and puts them into their shoebox before tiptoeing out of our bedroom.

The door closes quietly.

I wait a minute and then, leaving Jake snuggled in bed, sneak out onto the landing and peek through the bars of the staircase and down into the living room. To my surprise Marge is standing in the hallway, wide awake, with a clean face, and looking sensible with all her magical hair hidden away!

I peer closer and see Archie's green

blanket stuck to Marge's back like a cape.

That's why we couldn't find her – Marge must have crept off to sleep in Archie's doggy bed!

I snort back a giggle. I guess being small can be useful when it comes to finding comfy places to nap!

'How were they?' Daddy asks.

'The kids ate all their dinner, even the broccoli, and Jake's hair is clean,' Marge says proudly.

'Thank you!' Mummy says happily.

'It was easier washing my albino water buffalo's tail than Jake's hair though,' Marge says seriously, but Mummy and Daddy laugh, thinking that she is making a joke.

Jake and I both know that she's not!

When I'm back in our room I wriggle under my covers and sigh in wonder.

'Are you awake, Jakey?' I ask.

'Almost,' he says sleepily.

'Do you think Marge is a real duchess?' I ask.

Jake doesn't answer for a long time. Then I hear a giggle.

'Yes.'

'Why are you laughing?' I ask.

'We have a royal babysitter,' he says. 'But we have to babysit her!'

Jake's right, and it makes me smile. 'I hope that she comes again,' I reply, snuggling into my pillow.

Jake and I are silent, thinking about it for a moment.

'Do you think Mummy would buy me some rainbow hair dye? Jakey, what do you think?' I ask.

But there is only the soft sound of his breathing.

'Night-night, Jakey,' I whisper, and I turn out my light and drift off to sleep.

Marge at the Birthday Party

Hi! Remember me? I'm Jemima Button. I am seven years old and still the tallest in my class – though Rosie Williams is catching up with me now.

It's nine o'clock on Saturday morning. Jakey and I are downstairs eating eggs and soldiers. Jake is secretly feeding our puppy Archie all the runny yellow part of the egg, which he calls the 'yuk' instead of the 'yolk'. I have finished mine and now I'm drawing a picture of Granny's tabby cat George, who looks like an old man with a yellow beard.

Today I have butterflies in my tummy because Marge, our amazing babysitter, is taking us to Theo's party. Theo is Jake's best friend from school. He has one long eyebrow and always shares his snacks with Jake. Even though I am very excited to see Marge, I won't know anyone at the party, I will be the oldest child there and possibly the only girl! What if no one plays with me?

Mummy and Daddy can't come because they have to drive a long way today to visit Auntie Sally, who has had a new little baby. I'd love to meet baby Zara but I get carsick.

'Are you two going to be on your best behaviour for Marge today?' asks Daddy.

Jake and I share a hidden smile and nod our heads.

We can't promise that Marge will be on her best behaviour! She always seems sensible until Mummy and Daddy leave and then we end up having so much fun and making up our own rules to add to Mummy's list. Marge is secretly a duchess who used to live in a huge royal palace. But she hung up her tiara to live a life of incredible adventures. Anyway, she couldn't fit all her extraordinary pets into the palace stables!

DING DONG
Marge is here!

We jump up and run for the door.

Jakey beats me there and pulls it open. Our babysitter smiles from the doorstep.

'Look, I had a splinter yesterday!' cries my little brother. He lifts up his foot for Marge to see the scratch on his heel. 'Daddy took it out with tweezers and I didn't even cry,' he brags.

'Very brave,' says Marge, pinching his chubby cheeks. Jake never allows anyone else to do that!

Today Marge looks even smaller than I remembered. Can grown-ups shrink? She's wearing a smart jacket, stripy leggings and a tall hat to hide her long rainbow hair.

'*Buongiorno!*' Marge smiles at me. 'That is how Italian people say hello!'

Jake and I start to giggle.

'He-ll-o,' Jakey replies in his robot voice. 'Buon-gior-no . . .'

'The rules are on the fridge,' Mummy tells Marge as she fishes in her handbag for the car keys. Looking at us, she adds: 'Remember to be polite and say "please" and "thank you" when Marge takes care of you.'

Daddy is heading towards the door. 'Be good, you two. Enjoy the party.'

'I won't know anyone there!' I gulp.

'Parties are a great opportunity to make friends,' Daddy says.

'Take a book to read,' Mummy offers, trying to be helpful.

I imagine myself sitting reading, away from everyone else playing and having fun at the party. It makes me feel sad.

Mummy and Daddy give Jake and I both a big kiss.

We stand on the doorstep waving them goodbye. As soon as the car disappears, Marge turns to me.

'Do you see this?' She shows me a tiny silver necklace with half a loveheart. I hold it in my fingers. There is small writing engraved on it. It reads: *Best Friends Forever*.

'This is a friendship necklace, given to me by Chester.'

'Who is Chester?' I ask.

Marge settles into Daddy's brown armchair and we come in close to listen to her story. Marge tells the best stories.

'I met Count Chester, the meerkat, at an amazing party. There were balloon elephants and fire jugglers and I somehow got stuck in a giant bubble! Count Chester used his tiny claws to poke a Marge-sized hole in the bubble and set me free.'

SIR PADDINGTON'S PARTY
"Set me free!!"

Jake and I are open-mouthed.

'We became best friends for life!' Marge smiles.

Marge slips off her jacket to reveal a black T-shirt with a lightning bolt across the middle and takes off her tall hat and out tumbles a mass of rainbow-coloured hair. Now she is really here!

'Let's read that list. Hop to it!' Marge twirls towards the fridge, her tiny shiny shoes tapping on the kitchen floor as she whirls. She reminds me of a coloured spinning wheel.

'Today I can only read upside down,' she announces, bending over as she reads:

1. Theo's present is in the top drawer – please wrap

2. Party is at 11 o'clock in Heath Park

3. Only one slice of cake at the party

Marge finds Mummy's fountain pen by the phone.

She crosses out 'only one slice' and writes NINE slices of cake.

'Yay!' yells Jake.

'Marge is in charge!'

'Let's not fill up on too much healthy food today. We need to leave plenty of room for cake!' Marge says, laughing. 'Let's get started,' she adds, so I show her the drawer with the present. It is a giant plastic water pistol!

'Ohh, let's open it now!' Marge suggests and Jakey grins and claps his hands.

'I don't think we should,' I warn them. 'Theo won't want a birthday present that's already been played with.'

Oh no! Marge is already breaking the rules. I feel knots in my belly – I don't want to get into trouble with Mummy.

But Marge is holding the box and looking really excited. 'At the palace we had an official toy tester whose job was to make sure all the toys work before they are given as gifts! Today we can be the toy testers!'

'Fantastico,' Jakey agrees, nodding. Jakey

only says 'Fantastico' whenever something truly amazing happens. Like the time he won a competition for eating the most strawberry shoelace candy.

I can't help but smile. Toy testers? I guess that makes sense. Marge has already succeeded in cheering me up.

Marge grins and adds a new rule to Mummy's list.

Have a water fight before the party

We open the box and fill up the water pistol. But we don't fill it with water – we fill it with apple juice, because Marge says then we can take a sip if we get thirsty. Marge puts on her sunglasses.

'I don't want juice in my eyes,' she explains. 'I have very sensitive eyes. At the palace, I used to polish the tiny emeralds and rubies on the Queen's crown because my eyes were able to see even the tiniest fleck of dust.'

When the apple-juice pistol is ready I want to take a turn first because I am the eldest, but Jakey grabs it from me.

'Hey,' I say, and I snatch it back and then Jakey gets mad and pulls my hair!

OUCH. It really hurts. Mummy normally puts Jakey on time out when he is naughty but she isn't here and my eyes begin to fill with tears.

'Jake!' Marge scolds, peering over the top of her sunglasses. 'If anyone used their arms and legs to get their own way at the palace, they were made to trim all the hedges in His Majesty's gardens with nail scissors!'

Jake looks surprised. 'Nail scissors are tiny. And hedges are huge!'

'Exactly,' says Marge. 'Please apologise.'

'I'm sorry, Jemima,' my little brother says quietly. And would you believe that he gives me a hug? I ruffle his blond hair affectionately. I can't help it – no matter what my brother does, I love him so much.

Then we have the most amazing juice-gun fight . . .

SPLISH! goes the juice on my dress!

SPLASH! goes the juice on Jake's jumper!

We end up wrestling on the carpet and Archie starts chasing his tail and barking! I don't think I have ever laughed so hard in my life. Eventually Marge decides it's time to get ready, and we have to wash our hands and faces because of the apple juice.

Now my little brother has two rules (as well as no-broccoli-eating or hair-washing):

1. He won't wear a hat (even in the summer)

2. He never washes his face — EVER

But, would you believe it, when Marge asks him, he washes his face and even uses soap — **wow!**

He looks very pleased with himself as well.

Back in the living room, Marge notices the gold shiny wrapping paper for wrapping

Theo's birthday present.

'Ooh, that paper would make lovely party hats,' she says. 'Party hats are incredibly useful. All good parties end in a cake fight and party hats will protect our hair!'

So we make hats and as we cut and glue Marge tells us the best story ever. It is about a spectacular cake fight that happened on her last birthday. At the end of the fight, she was covered in a twelve-tier pink sponge cake with chocolate mousse icing.

'There was cake wedged in butler Jones's reading glasses and I had chocolate mousse up my nose and behind my ears for a week, and all because we didn't have hats!'

I most definitely do not want cake up my nose! I once got a frozen pea stuck up there and Mummy made me blow my nose until it popped out. It really hurt.

Even though Mummy never lets Jakey use the grown-up scissors, Marge does, but she stands by his side the whole time. Jake cuts out three crowns from the shiny paper very carefully, with his tongue poked out in concentration, and I paste glitter, jewels and beads onto them.

Marge ties the hats on with string. We

look like three glorious kings as we parade around the whole house! I still can't believe that Jake has agreed to wear a hat. As we parade around, Marge sings us a song:

'Off we go now
Hear us sing
Wearing crowns
We'll visit the king!'

WOOF?

I dance around like a ballerina while Jake follows, banging a wooden spoon as loudly as he can on a saucepan. Marge tells us that the last time she was in a royal procession she was nine years old.

'I secretly untied the Grand Duke's boot laces as he marched across the drawbridge and he tripped over and landed in the moat!'

Jakey thinks this is hilarious.

I am curious. 'Was the Duke cross with you?'

'No! He had a lovely swim with the royal swans. Swans are very snuggly, you know, because of their long necks.'

I try to picture cuddling a swan and it makes me laugh again. I bet Marge was a very naughty child, like Jakey.

At last we come to rest in the living room.

'What will we wrap Theo's water pistol in now?' I ask.

Marge closes her eyes and says in a serious voice:

*'Hocus pocus
help me to focus!'*

Then she reaches into her bag and a long yellow silk scarf appears magically! She ties an enormous bow around Theo's present.

'Harry Houdini taught me how to tie a bow like that,' Marge says.

'Who's Harry Houdini?' Jake and I ask in unison.

'The world's greatest magician. He could disappear and reappear from anywhere.'

'Archie our puppy does that at the park!' says Jake.

We all look at Archie and decide that he must be a magical dog.

Marge tips her head upside down and consults Mummy's list again.

'It says to arrive at the party at eleven o'clock.'

Jakey and I look up at the clock. The big hand is on the six and the little hand is on the ten. I count on my fingers.

'Marge, that's in half an hour,' I say.

'No, that's in twenty hours,' Jake says, correcting me. Marge and I exchange a look. Jakey hasn't learned to tell the time yet but we don't want to embarrass him.

'Let's get dressed,' says Marge. 'All parties have a dress code. Usually something very bright and special for birthdays.' She leads us upstairs to our bedroom, two steps at a time. Our puppy Archie chases after us, and Marge explains that the dressing-up includes him too!

Archie's furry head is cocked to one side. I think he can understand English, but no one except Jakey believes me.

'I don't think dogs are invited,' I say.

Marge is riffling through my closet but pauses to protest. 'Dogs love parties and birthday cake as much as people do, although you must always brush their fangs with mint toothpaste afterwards.

So we decide on my green lace dress for Archie. It's too big, but I have to admit the colour really suits him.

I put on my best dress. It's bright pink. Jakey lets me dress him in the blazer he got from Granny at Christmas. He even manages to do both buttons up!

After we are dressed Marge
tells us that no party is complete
without a lot of balloons! Inside Marge's
magical bag is a large packet, all in different
colours. So we sit in a circle huffing and
puffing and blowing up as many
balloons as we can. I choose the
blue and red ones and Jake blows
up the yellow and green and Marge
blows up two at a time of any colour she can
find! After a few minutes her face is as red
as a tomato and Jakey is panting so
much that it's making me laugh.

'Let's let them go,' says
Marge, watching hers
float up to the ceiling.

The balloons get bigger and bigger
and we blow up more and more. Soon our
living-room ceiling is hidden in rainbow
bubbles. There are so many balloons
I almost can't see
Jakey or Marge!

'I once got my feet tangled in fifty balloons and floated all the way to Wimbledon,' Marge declares, popping her head out between the balloons. 'My hairdo was completely ruined in the wind and everyone saw my knickers! It was embarrassing.'

Jake grabs a purple balloon and sits on it like a whoopee cushion. **POP!**

We all giggle.

'Marge . . .' I say, looking at the clock again, 'I think it's time to go!' I hate being late.

We leave the house with Archie dragging his dress behind him and an enormous cloud of rainbow balloons all bobbing and bumping into each other above our heads! I start to feel nervous again.

I have brought my book with me, just in case I get bored or lonely.

Theo's party is under the big oak tree in the little park near our house. It has been decorated with streamers and a banner reading 'FIVE YEARS OLD TODAY'. There is a chequered tablecloth laid out over a wooden bench covered with cupcakes and sandwiches and a big pile of presents. Behind the bench is a giant bouncy castle.

Now if there is one thing Jakey and I really love in the world it is bouncy castles. I wish my whole bedroom was a bouncy castle and that the bottom of my tennis shoes were made of bouncy castle too!

All the little boys are very happy to see Jakey and they say hi to us. I notice a few of them have their big siblings with them too. Josh's big sister Posy is here and Lucy Walker as well. I feel much much better seeing other girls my age at the party. Everyone laughs when they see Archie in a dress, particularly Theo! Theo doesn't even mind when Archie manages to steal a peanut butter cupcake.

'Happy Birthday, Theo!'

Marge, Jakey and I chorus as we hand over his present. Theo looks surprised by the yellow bow.

'Don't worry,' Marge tells him, 'we tested the water pistol out for you. It's ready to use and full up with apple juice!'

'Thanks!' says Theo, taking in Marge's height. 'Are you a child or a grown-up?' he asks, which makes me giggle.

Jakey explains very politely that Marge is actually a small grown-up. But that she is tall enough to ride a bike without training wheels, which is the only thing that matters.

Just as we take off our shoes to go onto the bouncy castle, disaster strikes! The sky clouds over and it starts to rain. At first it's just the pitter-patter of little drops but soon they turn into big fat blobs of water. Theo looks like he might cry. I would be really disappointed too if it were my birthday.

Theo's mummy explains that we can't go onto the bouncy castle when it's wet as it's too slippery and slidey. 'We don't want anyone bumping heads,' she says.

But Marge has the most brilliant idea. 'Marge to the rescue!' she calls as she gathers all the balloons we brought with us.

She ties them into a vast bundle, so big and thick it makes a roof for the bouncy castle. No rain can get in at all!

All the parents clap and cheer. I feel so proud that we brought Marge to the party and that she is our babysitter.

'Everyone on the bouncy castle,' Theo's mummy shouts and we all scramble up excitedly. Even Archie scampers up with us.

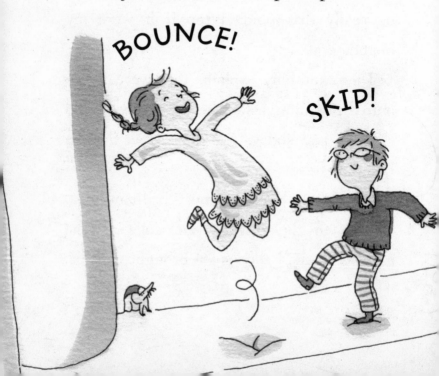

BOUNCE!

SKIP!

His furry ears flap as he gets bounced up and down.

What fun! Whenever I am on a bouncy castle I imagine what it would be like to be a bird and be able to fly. Jakey is jumping so high his trousers keep slipping down!

HOP!

JUMP!

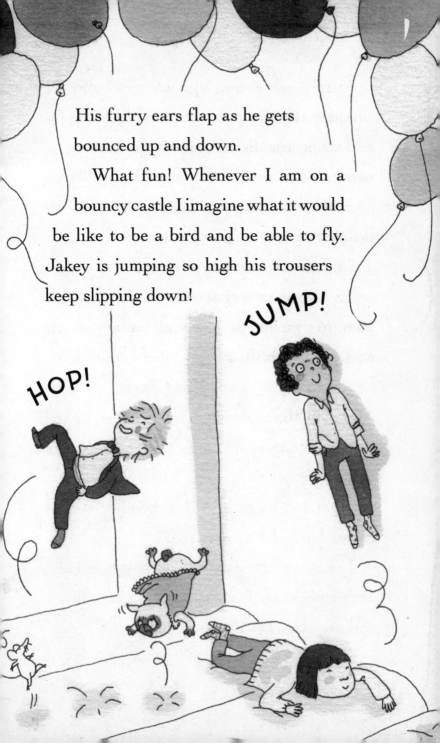

After a while our legs are tired and we sit down in the bouncy castle looking for something else to do. But it's still raining so we can't run around in the park yet. Theo's mummy and daddy are looking anxious – all the party plans are going wrong.

I am just about to ask everyone if they want me to read them a chapter from my book but then Marge jumps into the bouncy castle with another brilliant idea.

'By day I am Magnificent Marge, Masterful Babysitter of Jemima and Jakey Button. But by night I am . . . Magical Marge the Magician!'

What is Marge up to? I wonder. We all crowd around Marge to see.

'I need a drum roll,' she says dramatically. Theo's big sister Lucy is standing next to me and she claps her hands as loudly as she can.

I join in and soon everyone is clapping.

Marge twirls round and loses her balance on the grooves in the bouncy castle, her skinny legs buckling, but recovers quickly. Theo's little brother Matthew tries not to giggle.

Then Marge does a loud fake cough, covering her mouth with her hand, and when she pulls it away, there is . . . a purple silk handkerchief!

'Abra-ca-zebra!' she cries, looking very pleased with herself. 'Now, this looks like an ordinary handkerchief, but look again.'

We peer closely at the purple handkerchief. There is nothing weird about it, but then . . .

Marge's nose begins to twitch and she emits an enormous sneeze.

The birthday boy is unimpressed. Theo says, 'You don't need to be a magician to sneeze!'

But Marge smiles mysteriously and blows into the handkerchief as if it were a balloon. Then she shakes the purple silk and lo and behold, out fly twenty pink lollipops!

Everyone grabs one. Mine tastes of watermelon which is my favorite flavour for lollipops, even though I don't like the actual fruit.

Then Marge enlists the help of Archie as her magician's assistant! For her second trick she pulls a peanut butter cupcake out of her hat and then eats it using no hands, with Archie helping by licking up the crumbs.

'How did you learn magic?' Theo's friend Jack wants to know.

'Are you ready for a long story?' Marge replies.

We sit happily in a circle around Marge. Lucy sits next to me which is nice and we share a shy smile.

'One day a magician called Eduardo Alberti appeared at the palace to do magic for the whole village. As he was preparing for his grand show his assistant was trampled by a herd of pink flamingos. So he picked me and my twin sister Midge to be his assistants!'

Marge has a twin sister called Midge? I can't wait to meet her.

'What did you have to do?' asks Theo, his eyes as wide as saucers.

'Eduardo hid me in a box so you could only see my head and shoulders, and Midge in the other half of the box so you could only see her knees and legs – and then he sawed us in half!'

We all scream in unison.

'Show me how to do the tricks,' begs Theo.

'As a member of the Magic Triangle,' Marge says seriously, 'I am sworn to secrecy.'

Jakey and I can't believe it.

Marge has led the most incredible and amazing life of any grown-up we know!

Next up she juggles three balloons – well, she starts juggling with five, but one floats away and another pops when Archie bites it.

'Now for my final trick,' Marge says as she produces a deck of cards with a flourish. Suddenly she throws them into the air and sings:

♫ 'Cards, cards fly up in the air, ♪
♩ Make the weather fine and fair.
On this magical birthday,
Send the rain far away!'

We all scamper around catching the cards as they fall about us. I reach high to catch the ace of hearts.

'Look!' shouts Lucy.

We stare up at the sky. Would you believe that it has completely stopped raining? I look at Jake's face. His eyes are bulging in disbelief. Is Marge a real magician? We scramble out of the castle and back into our socks and shoes. The boys all take off, stretching their little legs and hollering with joy.

But now there seems to be another problem. Theo's father takes a phone call, then switches off his phone. He does not look happy.

'The face painter's car has broken down in a big puddle. He can't come.'

Marge doesn't need to be asked twice. 'Luckily . . .' she announces gallantly, 'I was taught face painting by one of the princess's ladies in waiting, and I am actually very good.'

She reaches into her bag and brings out some make-up and pens. We form a queue around the bouncy castle waiting for our turn.

I am a little hesitant to have Marge paint my face as she once tried to use Mummy's hair dye as a face mask!

She draws white make-up and pink lipstick on Lucy's face. 'You are Mary Antoinette, the French queen!' Then she paints my eyes with black eyeliner, which tickles at the beginning but then feels kind of nice, and my lips bright red.
'You are Cleopatra!'

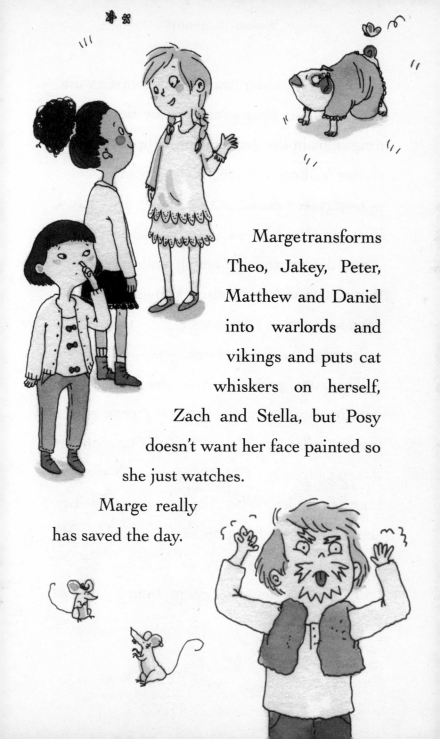

Marge transforms Theo, Jakey, Peter, Matthew and Daniel into warlords and vikings and puts cat whiskers on herself, Zach and Stella, but Posy doesn't want her face painted so she just watches.

Marge really has saved the day.

Lucy and I wander away from the party and take turns on the swing. I show her my red tongue from the watermelon lollipop and she shows me hers and we giggle.

Can you believe it that Lucy also has a little brother like me, she has also lost five teeth like me and she also has a secret diary that not even her mummy knows about. We have so much in common!

It's time for the party games.

The first game is Pass the Parcel. My mummy always makes sure everyone gets a present when we play this game on mine or Jakey's birthday. But Marge doesn't seem to know the rules. When the parcel reaches her, she just passes it from her left hand to her right hand until the music stops.

'I win!' she laughs, unwrapping a layer of paper.

'Marge!' I scold her. 'You have to share the present!'

'Sorry!' says Marge guiltily. 'When I lived in the palace, the King always let me win!' She hands the parcel along and Theo's little brother Matthew finally wins!

After the games, Theo's mummy calls out: 'Everyone sit down, please!'

It's time to sing 'Happy Birthday' to Theo and eat cake, so we find a place to sit cross-legged in front of the picnic bench.

'Happy Birthday to you,
Happy Birthday to you,'

we all sing. Jakey's voice is the loudest as he hugs his best friend Theo.

Looking at Theo's big chocolate cake with five candles on it, I feel very hungry.

I sometimes wish, when I see a big cake like that, that I could stick my whole face into it and gobble it all up. But I remember to sit nicely as I lick my lips and wait patiently.

Just as the cake is placed in front of Theo and he draws in a big gulp of air to blow out the candles, Marge pops her head up and blows them out first!

Oh no! I think.

Silence. Everyone stops singing Happy Birthday. No one has ever blown out the candles before except the birthday person. What bad manners!

Theo looks like he might be about to cry.

But suddenly the five candles re-light, and we all gasp.

Candles re-lighting by themselves?

'What happened?' asks Theo. He looks confused.

'It's because YOU are a secret magician,' Marge tells Theo.

'But I have never been a magician before,' Theo says.

'I made the wish for you,' Marge explains, 'when I blew out the candles. That's my birthday present for you. Candle wishes always come true.'

Theo gives a big puff and blows out the flames!

Whoopee!

Theo looks very happy, as though being a magician might be the best birthday present ever. Everyone claps and cheers and all the grown-ups take photos on their phones.

'How did you do that, Marge?' I whisper.

'It's just a trick!' Marge winks. 'A trick that I can't reveal unless you are a member of the Magic Square, which I am.'

'I think it's called the magic circle?' corrects Josh.

'Possibly,' concedes Marge.

Secretly I make a wish that Marge will always be our babysitter.

After this we all get stuck into the food and Marge says that the children are allowed nine slices of cake each, but after the sandwiches and crisps and fruit salad and sweets and nuts and popcorn I am too full to eat more than three slices of birthday cake and Jake only manages one (very big) one.

Marge reaches into her bag and pulls out her gold paper crown that we made earlier.

'So no one throws cake at me,' she whispers to Lucy and we laugh.

'I am going to nap before the cake fight starts,' Marge yawns. 'You know, Countess La Roo was able to marry off her two daughters by teaching them magic,' our babysitter warbles as she curls up with Archie. And there she lies, her feet poking out from behind the bouncy castle. Her gold crown is lopsided and her face paint is smeared. But she is sound asleep. Lucy and I decide she looks adorable.

'Shh,' says Lucy. 'She needs her sleep after all that work. How old do you think Marge is?'

'Jake thinks that she is one hundred and fifty-one,' I whisper and we head over to where the other kids are playing.

I have a fantastic time playing with Theo, Jakey and Lucy. We play Follow the Leader, with me and Lucy at the front and all the younger children following, until we arrive at the swings. Then Jake and Theo take turns pushing all of us back and forth.

HONK HONK!

I can hear Daddy's horn!

I look over and see Mummy and Daddy getting out of the car.

'*Buongiorno!*' I say as I run and give them a hug. They look exhausted from their long drive.

'How was the party?' asks Daddy.

'I made a new friend called Lucy,' I tell Mummy.

'That's great, Jemima! Well done,' says Mummy.

'It was the best party ever!' says Jakey.

We all thank Theo and his parents for a wonderful time and when Marge reappears with her hair tucked away and looking very sensible, they thank her for saving the day.

'I can't believe that Jakey wore a hat!' Daddy says when he hears about Jake's paper crown.

Then Mummy notices Archie.

'Is that your party dress, Jemima?' she asks me.

'Yes, Archie needed to be properly dressed to be a magician's assistant,' Marge explains.

Mummy and Daddy exchange a look.

'What a clever puppy putting it on all by himself. Amazing paw control!' Daddy jokes.

'He's the real Harry Houdini!' says Jake proudly and we all laugh and laugh.

Marge at Large in School

Hi, Jemima Button here, with my little brother Jakeypants. There are lots of things that Jake and I don't agree on – like Jake prefers the shallow end of the pool and I like to swim in the deep end and I always eat sweets slowly to make them last and he gobbles them up in one go. But we both love to sit by the square window that looks down over our driveway. We call it the 'spying window'. Sometimes we spy on the neighbours walking their dog and sometimes we count how many green bins there are on our street, but right now we are waiting for someone.

Marge, our royal babysitter and favourite

grown-up (after Mummy and Daddy) is coming to take us to school today.

We are going to jump out and surprise her!

Even though it's seven o'clock on Monday morning and I have PE after lunch, I am still so excited because I love Marge. I love Marge as much as I hate PE (I'm the third slowest runner in our class).

As Marge's mint-green Mini Cooper screeches into the driveway, my heart is racing.

'In position!' Jake shouts.

We run downstairs and Jakeypants and I hide behind the front door. I have a sofa cushion as a weapon and he has a pillow. Our puppy Archie is with us as well and he keeps panting loudly.

'Shhh,' I tell him, 'or you'll have to hide somewhere else!

Marge can't know that we are here.' We wait, holding our breath. Her footsteps get closer. **DING DONG**, that's the doorbell!

Jake and I squeeze further back against the wall. The door handle turns.

Marge steps into the doorway. 'Hell-ooooo,' she calls to the empty hallway.

Jakey and I shout, **'ATTACK!'** and we both jump onto Marge.

I cling onto her back and Jakey throws his pillow first and then grabs her leg. Archie barks and wags his tail in excitement.

'Argh!' screams Marge in surprise as she flies forward onto the carpet. I wrestle her but she is so small and quick that she manages to roll away from us like a ninja.

'It's Marge the tickle monster,' she calls and begins tickling my chest and Jakey's feet. I throw a pillow at her head but she ducks.

We can't stop laughing and Archie is yapping at us all mangled in a heap.

'Kids, get off Marge right now, please.' Daddy sounds cross as he passes through the hallway into his office.

Jakey and I spring to our feet as Mummy appears in the hallway.

'Sorry, Marge!' Mummy apologises. She makes a stern 'we'll talk about this later' face at us.

But Marge is smiling as Mummy helps her to her feet. Marge is wearing a blue skirt with a beret, which is a kind of French hat that makes adults look silly.

'The list of things to remember is on the kitchen table,' Mummy says, grabbing Daddy's glasses for him, which he always forgets.

As Mummy gives Jake and me a quick kiss goodbye she says, 'Remember to be polite and say "please" and "thank you" when Marge takes care of you. And no more wrestling the babysitter!'

'Have you seen my glasses?' Daddy calls.

'I have them,' Mummy replies as they both head out the door.

'Bye, kids. Have fun at school,' our parents call as the door slams.

We run back upstairs and wave them goodbye from the spying window. When their car is as small as an ant Marge turns to us.

'Bonjour,' she sings as she pulls off her French beret and out tumbles her rainbow hair.

Holy hamburger!

It is plaited into a million tiny coloured braids with little bows on the end.

'*Bonjour* means hello in French. Now lets take a squiz at this list.'

I fetch the list and bring Mummy's fountain pen too as I know that Marge likes to add new rules of her own.

The list says:

1. Breakfast

2. Pack school lunches

3. Jakey must wear new school shoes

4. Drop off at school at 8 o'clock

'What's for breakfast?' Marge asks, swanning into the kitchen. 'I'm feeling a little peckish – what are you both making me? Hop to it!'

Jakey looks at me with one eyebrow raised. I giggle.

'Marge, you are the grown-up! YOU are supposed to be making breakfast for us!' I explain.

'Oh!' Marge is surprised. 'I've never made breakfast before. The Queen's cook Mabel used to bring me breakfast in bed every morning,' Marge says wistfully.

I am curious. 'What did Mabel make you?'

'Royal Pancakes,' Marge sniffs, 'with extra syrupy syrup.'

'I love pancakes,' Jake says. 'I'm hungry!'

My tummy is grumbling too. What are we going to do about breakfast?

'I am sure that I can make you a pancake,' Marge announces confidently. 'How hard can it be? If Mabel can do it, so can Marge!' She takes Mummy's pen and adds *Royal Pancakes* to the first rule. 'Marge's marvellous pancakes with extra syrupy syrup coming right up!'

Marge begins by rummaging around the kitchen in search of a pan and a bowl.

'You really don't have a butler or a chef to help me?' asks Marge after a while.

I giggle and shake my head. I wish we didn't have to go to school today. Spending time with Marge is so much fun!

I help Marge and together we mix some eggs and butter, flour and milk into a batter and Jake whisks it up. Then Marge turns on the stove.

'Back away, little servants,' Marge hollers as flames lick the giant pan. 'I don't want to burn down the kingdom!'

Jake and I step away as Marge pours the entire mixture into the pan.

'I am actually making crêpes which is French for pancakes. They taste even more delicious,' Marge exclaims.

'Don't you want to use the spatula thing that flips the pancakes?' I squint at Marge. 'That's what Mummy uses.'

'Nonsense. Mabel the royal cook never needed to rely on fancy utensils.
I am just going to toss it into
the air like . . . THIS!'

Marge grabs the pan with both hands and tosses the pancake high into the air. Jake and I watch as it flies up, up, up and sticks **SPLAT** onto the ceiling!

'Call the guards, shut the drawbridge – we have a runaway pancake!' shouts Marge urgently.

I don't know what to think. The pancake is stuck on the ceiling and it doesn't look like it's going anywhere.

'I think we should call the fire department,' Jakey suggests. 'They have a big ladder that we can climb up to reach it.'

'That's silly,' I say. 'The fire department can only come for emergencies.'

'This is most definitely an emergency,' Marge says gravely.

We all stare at the pancake for a few moments, thinking. Then Marge suggests that we should just wait for it to drop back down into our mouths and catch it like Archie catches his ball.

But after we have waited for a while with our mouths wide open, my jaw is beginning to ache. 'I'm so hungry and tired,' complains Jake.

'Maybe it's still cooking,' Marge offers hopefully.

'On the ceiling?' I ask.

Just when we are close to giving up and getting some cereal instead, gravity gets the better of the pancake.

PLOP!

Down it falls and lands right in the middle of Marge's head!

'Breakfast is served! Tuck in,' Marge says.

We grab forks and Marge pours syrup all over her head and we eat it right off her hair in big gooey gulps! Jake is so hungry he ends up gobbling up half the pancake so I have to stop him before he eats any of Marge's multi-coloured hair!

'Here!' Jakey grabs Marge's beret. 'I think

you need to put your hat back on, your hair looks very sticky!'

Marge reads Rule Two aloud in a French accent: 'Pack school lunches.'

I show her where Mummy keeps our lunchboxes in the fridge. She looks suspiciously at the sandwiches, sniffing the bread and cheese. In the end she decides that they are delicious and healthy but that we must have treats too. So she fills the rest of our lunchbox with chocolate sprinkles from the baking drawer.

I grin and Jake claps his hands. 'Marge is in charge!' he declares.

Marge consults the list again. 'Now for Rule Three: Jake, Mummy says you have to wear your new school shoes.'

Jakey looks furious.

His little face has turned red like a traffic light. 'I hate wearing shoes!' he yells.

'All shoes?' asks Marge.

'Yes,' replies Jake. He looks determined.

So Marge runs out of the room and returns five minutes later with a big brown sack that she has collected from the hallway closet.

'Ta-da,' she says. 'It's Super Marge to the rescue!'

She turns the sack upside down and pours out a mountain of shoes. There are hiking boots, roller skates, clown shoes, flippers, stilts, skis and even a pair of ice skates!

'Do any of these look fun?' she asks my brother.

'I wanna wear the roller skates!' Jake says, grinning.

Marge laces them up.

'But I don't know how to roller skate!' confesses Jake.

'Don't worry,' Marge replies. 'They can teach you at school!'

'Let's bring your school shoes too, just in case,' I say sensibly, packing them in his rucksack.

'From what I've heard they can teach you everything at school,' Marge says. 'I would love to go myself one day.'

'Didn't you have to go to school when you were a kid?' I ask Marge.

Marge pauses to think for a moment, then curls into Daddy's armchair, which I am beginning to think of as Marge's story chair.

'Are you ready for a story?' Marge asks.

I love it when Marge tells us stories from her days at the palace. Marge gave up her life as a duchess because she hates rules. If you think living in a normal house has lots of rules, imagine living in a palace! But I don't want *too* long a story now because we have to go to school soon and I hate being late.

'Prince Rupert and I had a governess called Lady Morag. A governess is like a teacher for the royal family. She had pointy teeth and she made us practise piano until our fingertips were sore.'

PIANO CLASS.
With ~~Governess~~ Lady Morag
DRAGON

Oh no! Jakey and I share a look. She sounds terrifying. Poor Marge.

'One day Prince Rupert and I had had enough. We tricked Lady Morag into the dungeon and then locked her in with the rats and cobwebs.'

Jake claps his hands with glee, but I think the palace dungeon sounds scary. Marge seems to understand.

'We let her out again, of course,' she explains. 'It wasn't for long, but she learned her lesson. Lady Morag was much nicer to all the royal children after that!'

Marge stands up and we head to the door.

Suddenly Jakey's bottom lip starts to quiver and he bursts into tears. 'I don't want to go to school today!' he sniffs.

I know why my little brother is upset so I tell Marge. 'We are practising for the school concert first, before class.'

Jakey and I share music rehearsals with some of the other classes on Monday mornings. I like the practices but Jake says they are lame. He does not enjoy playing the recorder.

'It's BORING,' Jakey wails. 'I'm allergic to music.'

I give him a hug and try to cheer him up. 'You just have to practise the notes.'

Suddenly Marge springs to life and leaps onto the coffee table dramatically.

'By day, I am Magnificent Marge the Babysitter, but by night I am Marge the Musician.'

WOW! Marge is a musician too!

'I am the star of the Royal Brass Band,' Marge boasts.

'What's a brass band?' asks Jakey, his tears drying up.

'It's a group of musicians who all play brass instruments like trumpets, horns and the tuba,' explains Marge.

'Who is in the band with you?' I ask, imagining her princess friends.

'No one,' says Marge, 'I play all the instruments by myself. I like to promenade in the royal gardens wearing all of them around my neck.'

Jake seems to cheer up at this. 'Will you come to our school concert rehearsal?'

'Of course!' says Marge, gathering our schoolbags and putting her hat back on.

Phew, we are finally setting off for school!

It turns out roller skating is actually very hard! While Marge and I walk along the pavement chatting, Jakey's little legs pump faster and faster on the skates until we reach the top of a very big hill. After that he whizzes past us and disappears into some bushes! Extremely fast.

Marge and I look at each other, horrified. This reminds me of the time we lost Jakey at the supermarket when he was very small. He was finally discovered by Daddy lying under the shopping trolley, licking the wheels!

'Jakey?' I call, looking everywhere. I can't see him. My heart is starting to beat quicker. 'How will I tell Mummy that we lost Jakey?' I worry.

'He's not lost,' Marge explains. 'He's temporarily missing.'

We hear a scrabbling sound coming from the bushes. Then a brown squirrel darts out, followed by Jakey, who is covered in twigs and leaves. He grins from ear to ear. 'I love skating and I didn't even skin my knees!'

He's tired out, though, so I make him take the skates off and wear his school shoes. We are on our way to school again!

At the school gates our music teacher, Mrs Potts, is waiting to take the children to our music rehearsal. Marge introduces herself with an elaborate curtsy.

'How do you do? I was born Margery Beauregard Victoria Ponterfois and I . . . am a duchess.'

Mrs Potts seems quite surprised when Marge insists on attending the rehearsal, but after she points out that she is a musician herself in the Royal Brass Band, Mrs Potts allows her to come along.

I am slightly nervous about Marge being at school with us. What mischief will she create?

On the walk to the music hall I overhear Marge confiding in Mrs Potts, 'I've never been to a school before. My last governess taught me needlepoint and wild flower pressing!'

'You were home-schooled?' asks Mrs Potts.

'Palace-schooled,' corrects Marge.

Mrs Potts's mouth is open in surprise and Jakey and I can't help but stifle a giggle.

Everyone is staring at Marge as we enter the hall, as her beret hat is stuck on at a weird angle from all the syrup and she is doing an excited little jig on the spot.

Mrs Potts claps her hands twice for quiet and Jakey and I sit down with Rosie,

William, Lucy and Theo. They all remember Marge from Theo's party and wave hello. Marge stands at the front of the hall with our music teacher.

'Good morning, girls and boys,' says Mrs Potts. She smiles brightly as we all say good morning back to her (except for Jakey, who is looking nervously at the musical instruments in the corner).

'Meet Jemima and Jake's babysitter, Margery Beauregard Victoria . . . *Porcupine*?'

Everyone laughs.

'Er, sorry if I got that wrong,' says Mrs Potts. 'Anyway, Marge is going to help us today.'

Marge takes a bow as if she is being given an award, then dances from foot to foot as if the ground is boiling hot, which makes everyone laugh.

Mrs Potts is looking flustered again.

'Oh no,' she says, rummaging through her papers. She turns to Marge. 'It appears I've left the sheet music behind. I'll be right back. Will you watch the children until I return?'

Marge nods enthusiastically.

Jake and I exchange a look. I can't believe that Marge is in charge of an entire hall of children!

As soon as Mrs Potts has left, Judy Briggs puts her hand up. 'Are you a child or a grown-up?' she asks Marge. Everyone giggles again.

'Jake will explain,' Marge replies.

So Jakey stands up and politely tells the whole class that Marge is actually a very small grown-up. But that she is tall enough to reach the middle shelf of the fridge, the cheese shelf, which is all that matters. Jakey loves cheese as much as I love sticker books. Everyone nods in agreement.

'Let's begin class,' Marge announces in an important voice. 'I am your temporary governess so please line up while I hand out your musical instruments.'

Marge has found the big blue bucket in the corner filled with all the instruments and is standing by it proudly.

As we make a line in front of Marge I notice that some of the boys are taller then Marge, which makes me giggle.

Marge closes her eyes and fishes into the bucket as if it were a lucky dip.

There is a beat of silence before she says, '*Voilà!*' and pulls out a clarinet.

She hands it to Rosie Williams, who looks confused.

'But I play the violin,' Rosie says as the rest of the class laughs.

Marge thinks for a minute. 'Not today you don't. Everyone should learn how to play as many instruments as they want. How else will you find the ones you like the most? I myself have fourteen favourite instruments.

I am as accomplished on the French horn as I am on the Scottish bagpipes.'

Marge fishes back into the bucket.

'Next!' she calls.

Judy is next in the queue and is given a guitar instead of her flute, then it's Jakey's turn.

Marge fishes into the bucket, humming with her eyes closed, and pulls out a triangle.

'But I don't know how to play it!' Jakey worries. 'And if I am not very good on the recorder I will be terrible on the triangle.'

'Nonsense,' says Marge. 'Just listen to your heart and you will make wonderful music. NEXT!'

I am the next in the queue and Marge fishes out a trumpet. I love the sound that a trumpet makes but I have never thought to play it before because I usually play the violin, and no other girls in my year play the trumpet.

Suddenly I feel quite excited to
play a new instrument and I
put my mouth around the
end and blow –
PFF! A strange
raspy sound comes out.

One by one all the instruments get handed
out until nearly everyone has an instrument
that they have never played before. There
is a small tug-of-war over the drums that is
quickly resolved by Marge deciding that all
three boys can play them at the same time.

A handful of the younger children haven't
lined up for an instrument.

'We don't want to play anything,' Mary
Cooper complains. 'It's not fun.'

'I'm going to make a special
instrument just for you!'
Marge says cheerfully.

Marge busies herself in the corner. She fills an empty jam jar with paperclips, pins and staples and makes a colourful shaker.

'Ohh . . .' Mary looks thrilled as she makes a rattle sound with it.

So we all help to make instruments for other children without them. I find an empty coffee can and make a drum. Judy manages to make a rain stick for Harrison's little brother. Marge finds some old bells, ties them to pieces of ribbon and hands them out. Soon everyone is happy.

'Now we are ready for a concert!' cries Marge.

We're a little bit nervous, but gradually everyone starts playing.

'Close your eyes and make lots of noise! There is no wrong way to play music,' Marge says as she sways in front of us.

We are all blowing, banging, strumming, dancing, clapping and singing! The sound is so noisy that I can't hear my own trumpet even though it is very loud.

ZIIING

HONK

CLAC
CLAC

EEEE

I look over at Jake. He looks so happy as he dings the shiny metal triangle in time to the music.

'You all sound brilliant!' Marge says enthusiastically. 'Let's share our wonderful music with the rest of the school!'

Marge flings open the door and leads the entire classroom along the corridor and out into the playground.

Even though it sounds terrible we are all having so much fun. I now understand why music makes you feel happy, even though I can't make anything but a raspberry sound come out of this trumpet. Rosie is playing her clarinet like it's a guitar and Lucy is wearing a drum on her head.

'It's my drum hat,' she says and bangs it. It makes the funniest sound!

Theo is playing the violin backwards! But you won't believe this – he's actually making a good noise. Jake is tinging his triangle proudly in time to the music and Marge is singing like she is in an opera! Her voice is shaky and shrill like a lost goat on a mountain top.

We end up in the centre of the playground and we are making such a racket that all the other kids and teachers come out of their rooms and form an audience.

At first no one knows what to make of us but soon the other kids start tapping their feet and clapping along and the teachers find it impossible to disapprove as we are clearly having so much fun. Even Mrs Turnball, our strict science teacher, is nodding her head in time with the music, and some of the older kids are dancing!

My cheeks are hurting from blowing and laughing and everyone seems to love our crazy show!

I can't see Marge anywhere. Where is she?

Then I hear a deep sound and turn round. Marge is wearing Jakey's roller skates and has strapped a tuba to her neck. The tuba is like a trumpet for a giant and it is twice the size of her body! I have only seen an older girl called Martha play it once before.

Marge is blowing the tuba loudly and skating around us all.

Oh no, Marge, you have gone too far, I think. She is twirling way too fast as she sails past me.

Mr Lindon, our PE teacher, shouts, 'Watch out!' as Marge whizzes past him. But he is too late.

CRASH!
BANG!
SPLASH!

Marge has lost her balance and fallen face down into the little water fountain in the middle of the playground.

Zwiiiip!

We all can't stop giggling as Mrs Potts arrives back to see Marge upside down in the fountain with her head stuck inside the tuba and just her little legs poking out!

Everyone is laughing their heads off, but Jakey and I rush forward and help Marge out of the water. Jake and Theo take hold of the tuba and I grab her little feet, and try to pull her out of it. Then Rosie takes a hold of me and helps pull, and Lucy takes a hold of Rosie, and Jamie and Peter take a hold of Lucy, and before I know it all the pupils have lined up and are pulling like a tug of war to get Marge free from the tuba. Until . . .

POP!

Marge is free! We all fall down but no one is hurt and I'm relieved that Marge is okay, even if the tuba is a little wet.

'Well done, my fellow musicians!' Marge praises us, and we end up in a big group hug.

Just then Mr Siles, our headmaster, appears in the playground. 'All right, everyone, back to class,' he says sternly. He raises an eyebrow at the sight of Marge, soaking wet, in a beret, holding a tuba.

'Marge, it's time for lessons now,' I explain.

'Can I join your class?' she replies, running ahead to the classroom.

We all head back inside and the morning passes quickly. I can tell that everyone is in a good mood after our concert in the playground. Even Mrs Potts doesn't seem to mind about the tuba and in Maths Mr Bates gives us prizes for getting our answers right! I get the 'Star of the Day' certificate and Marge wins three gold stickers.

At breaktime Marge gives Jake, Theo, Jamie and Peter roller-skating lessons in the playground. Then in PE Marge convinces Mr Lindon that all throwing and catching should be done to music. It turns out that I never miss the ball when I am listening to Marge singing loudly, and for once I really enjoy PE!

In Art Marge suggests that we should finish our self-portraits blindfolded. I thought our art teacher, Mr Brock, was going to lose his temper when Ella painted on Drew's sweater by accident and James knocked over an entire pot of green paint . . . but by the end of class even Mr Brock agreed that everyone's portraits looked more unusual and that the exercise had 'unlocked our creativity'. It's so much fun having Marge at school!

BING! Now it's time for lunch.

We tidy up the art room and fetch our lunchboxes, ready to sit in our lunch circle. As I'm walking back to our classroom, Jakey pops up beside me. 'Mrs Potts said that I can join your class for lunch today because I was so well-behaved in music rehearsals.'

I can tell that Jakey is excited to see our babysitter again, and when we walk through the door we see that Marge is sitting in the middle of the floor. Jakey runs to give her a hug. Our form teacher, Mr Gale, looks a little surprised, but I don't think he minds.

'Could you look after the children while I eat my lunch in the staffroom?' he asks Marge.

'Of course!' Marge agrees, giving Jakey a big smile.

As we sit down in a circle around her, Marge brings out a lunchbox and a giant spoon from her handbag.

'In the palace we had an official food tester whose job was to make sure that no one poisoned the King or Queen!' She grins hopefully at us.

Everyone is happy to share a bite of their lunch with Marge.

One spoonful of Jack's jam sandwich . . .
YUM!

Two spoonfuls of Sarah's pasta . . .
TOO COLD!

Half of Rosie's peanut butter and apple . . .
TASTY!

ALL of Eli's fish fingers . . . **DELISH!**

Marge rubs her belly and sighs. 'In the palace, after lunch we always had nap time. A duchess can get very tired, you know.'

Marge stretches and snuggles into the beanbag in our library corner, next to her tuba.

'Will you read me a book?' she asks in a baby voice.

Lucy and I run and get our favourite storybook and Eli gets a blanket from the cupboard. When Marge is tucked up, we read her a bedtime story. Jakey is in charge of turning the pages and everyone joins in. We pass the book around the class and take it in turns to read a page each.

Once we have finished the story Marge's eyes are closing.

'Can you leave the light on?' Marge asks. 'I'm scared of ghosts.'

Jakey rolls his eyes. 'There is no such thing as ghosts! Even I know that and I'm only four.' He really is brilliant at eye rolling.

'Yes there are,' Marge replies. She pulls her blanket off and covers her head with it.

'**Whoooo!**' she calls in a ghostly voice. '**Whooo** . . .'

Everyone in the class starts to giggle. Marge is so funny.

'It's me, Marge the magnificent ghost!' she jokes.

Then Marge yawns sleepily, cuddles up to the tuba and promptly dozes off.

When he gets back from lunch Mr Gale is very impressed at how quietly we're sitting in our lunch circle. He doesn't seem to notice that Marge is asleep in the corner and we are only being quiet because we don't want to wake her up.

I can't stop thinking about Marge for the rest of the day. I go from class to class wondering if Marge is still asleep or if she is up to any more mischief. I wish I could peek in on her and see if she is still asleep on the beanbag but I don't have time and the day seems to whizz past.

BING!

That's the bell telling me that school is finished for the day!

At the school gates I find Mummy, Daddy and Jakey waiting for me.

'How was school, Jemima?' Daddy asks.

'I played the trumpet today!' I brag. 'And I didn't miss the ball once during throw and catch in PE.'

'How were music rehearsals for you, Jakey?' Mummy asks my little brother. She looks a little worried because he usually complains all the way home from school on Mondays.

'I LOVED music rehearsals,' Jakey says happily. 'Marge taught me to play the triangle and Mrs Potts said that because I like to play it so much I can play it again next week!'

'Marge was in school?' Mummy asks, surprised.

At that moment I hear a familiar sound and we all turn to look.

Marge is walking out of the school with the tuba around her neck playing a very loud tune. She gives us a big smile.

'I blew all the water out of it!' Marge announces. 'Mrs Potts says that I can join the school band too. I just need to practise a bit at home first,' Marge says excitedly.

Mummy and Daddy share a look as Jakey and I crack up laughing.

'Where's my horse and carriage to take us home?' Marge asks innocently.

'Very funny, Marge,' Daddy replies, pointing to our old blue car. Then he flings open the back door, bows down very low and cries, 'Your carriage awaits, Your Royal Highness!'

I'm giggling because Marge seems to bring out the funny side in everyone.

'*Merci!*' replies Marge in a posh voice. 'That is French for thank you,' she explains as we all bundle inside.

I can't help smiling all the way home as

Jake and I cuddle up with Marge on the back seat and Mum and Dad ask us questions about our day.

Who would have thought that our babysitter would need picking up from school too? Marge definitely isn't an ordinary grown-up, but to me she's the best babysitter in the whole wide world.